ON THE RUN

ON THE RUN

A DUTCH BOY
RESCUES AN AMERICAN
PILOT IN OCCUPIED
HOLLAND

Casey Willems

WALKA BOOKS

NEW ORLEANS

ON THE RUN A Dutch boy Rescues an American Pilot
 In Occupied Holland
© 2009 by Casey Willems

Walka Books
2709 Royal St
New Orleans LA 70117

Cover Photo: Ben Willems, Amersfoort, the Netherlands.

ISBN 13:   978-0-9722903-3-3
ISBN 10:   0-9722903-3-8

DEDICATION

For Conny...

Without whom there would be no book.

Acknowledgments

My sincere thanks for encouragement and support to Kate Barron, Charles Bohn, Teresa Brown, Mary Reidy, and Bob Weilbaecher.

Peggy Rosenfeldt was a tremendous editor.

Many thanks to my soul-mate and editor-in-chief, my wife Conny

Casey Willems
New Orleans, 2009

Foreword

Casey Willems was four years old when war came to his native Holland. Several decades later, he came to this country and worked in the hotel industry. It did not take long for the author to turn his hobby into a business, and he became well-known in New Orleans for his pottery.

Hurricane Katrina brought the people of New Orleans tragedy, confusion, hopelessness, the loss of homes, friends, and dislocation. But as in most dire situations, there were people who acted nobly. These events awoke slumbering memories in Mr. Willems of similar events, along with a resolve that what had happened to the people of Holland half a century before not be forgotten, particularly by younger generations.

For myself, this book covers familiar ground. I spent much time in the Netherlands both as a visitor and as a researcher. My first book was published there. Over many years I have become an admirer of the Dutch people and their nation, their struggles during the war years, and the way they keep those memories alive.

This book is an unusual departure for us. It is the first work of fiction, and the first book aimed at younger readers proudly published by Walka Books. This is a work of fiction, but it is also an accurate portrayal of life in the Netherlands during the last year of the war.

George F. Cholewczynski
Publisher, Walka Books

Chapter 1
PONIES

"Of course, I would love to do that!" Frans blurted out. He wanted to give Brother Bernard a big hug, but it didn't seem right to hug a clergyman, even when he had just made you the greatest offer in the world. Brother Bernard, one of the clergymen who ran the boarding school that Frans attended was in charge of the farm, including a band of ponies, and had just asked Frans if he would like to help him. Imagine taking care of seven ponies; who would not be elated just at the thought.

Frans had moved to the boarding school at the beginning of April, 1944. He came during the middle of the school year, because of the ongoing war. Frans felt lonely, for all the boys had already made friends and he felt himself an outsider. Taking care of the ponies would make him special.

On February 22, 1944, Nijmegen, the city where Frans lived, was accidently bombed by the Americans with devastating results. Through a number of navigational errors, Nijmegen was mistaken for a nearby German city. The center of the city was nearly obliterated. Almost 800 citizens died and hundreds more were wounded. Frans' uncle and a nephew were among the victims. People fled the city for safer places in the country, but Frans' parents had nowhere to go. They worried about their son's safety, and looked for a place where he would be out of harm's way. They found a boarding school in a small village in the eastern province of Overijssel near Zutphen that would take him. The school seemed big to Frans. It had over 300 students in grades one to eight. The move had not been easy for Frans, who did not like to live under strict rules.

"I will have to live with forty boys in a large hall and sleep in a large dormitory," Frans complained. "I'll have to wake up, eat, go to classes, do sports, and everything with everybody else. I'll have no room of my own. How can I read the books I like? What if the boys will tease me, or beat me up? You know I like to be by myself and read."

It was obvious that Frans didn't want to go, but his parents were adamant, realizing that it was safer for Frans to be away from the city, and off to boarding school he went. He would hate not being able to go outside after school, and play with his friends whom he had known all his life. He knew he would miss his Mom terribly, for she always listened to him and knew what to say when he had a problem.

On May 10, 1940, the German army, superior in

numbers and equipment, had attacked and overran the Netherlands. The Dutch army had taken a stand but was soon overpowered and Holland came under German control. As the occupation went on and on the Germans restricted more and more of the people's freedoms. Everybody fourteen years and older had, at all times, to carry identification papers. Men and boys between 18 and 50 years old, unless they had essential jobs, were sent to Germany to work on weapons production as unpaid laborers. Newspapers were censored; Frans' father complained that they did not publish the truth, but how, Frans wondered, would his Dad, or anybody else, know what the truth was. As time went on things only got worse.

For children life changed too. There was a shortage of food and Frans dreamt of the times when he could eat as much as he wanted, which seemed like a long time ago. School went on as before, although with many restrictions. There were curfews, not only for kids: nobody was allowed outside after dark. All windows were boarded up at night so that no light could be seen from the outside and airplanes would not be able to orient themselves. Since every radio was confiscated by the Germans even that simple pleasure was taken away.

"Be nice to the Germans," Frans was told by his parents.

"But everybody hates them," Frans answered.

"Perhaps most people do, but not everybody, and you do not know who does and who doesn't," warned his Dad, "in any case stay away from the Germans as much as possible."

The boarding school was in an 18th Century castle complete with turrets, located at the end of a long lane lined with elm trees. Farms and orchards dotted the landscape around it. The castle with its fields and forests was surrounded by a fence with a large front gate that almost never opened. Frans felt locked up.

So when Brother Bernard asked Frans to be his helper and take care of the ponies, it felt like the greatest thing that could ever happen to him.

"When can I start?" Frans asked.

"Tomorrow morning if you like," answered Brother Bernard, "but first we better go and talk to Brother Superior to see if he agrees. You won't be able to participate in all the scheduled activities, which I imagine you will surely miss." Frans was so excited that he was not sure whether he saw a twinkle in Brother Bernard's eye. That evening, after dinner, when all the boys were reading, playing chess or cards, Brother Bernard and Frans went to meet with Brother Superior.

From behind his imposing mahogany desk

Brother Superior said sternly, "I don't think it is right for one pupil to be excluded from all sports and other group activities."

"But I really need some help," Brother Bernard pleaded, "I am sure that Frans is the right person for the job. Could we try it for a while?" After some more discussion, Brother Superior finally agreed, and Frans almost hugged again, and this time not one, but two clergymen.

The next morning, even before breakfast was over, Brother Bernard, who had put a large apron over his dark brown habit, came to fetch Frans.

"I hope you put on your oldest clothes because you will have to work in the barn and some of the jobs are pretty dirty," Brother Bernard said. Frans looked confused.

"I have only two sets of clothes," he said, "except for my Sunday best. I will write my Mom to send some old ones, but with the war and all. . ." Frans held out his arms and shrugged forlornly.

"Don't worry," Brother Bernard said, "I do have an apron for sure, and hopefully I'll find a pair of *klompen* (wooden shoes) that might fit you." As they walked to the stables Brother Bernard told Frans about what was expected of him and explained the daily chores and the order in which they should be done. He emphasized that Frans had to make sure, above all, not to miss any classes and to be on time for all of them.

"You will be able to hear the bell for class and you better be there. Brother Superior surely does not want to hear any complaints from your teachers," he added.

Frans had seen the ponies many times before. The little horses were used to pull carriages over the grounds of the school as a form of entertainment for the boys. He knew them by name. Miep, the oldest with the sad eyes, looked like she still missed the little princesses of the Dutch royal family, who had learned to ride horseback on her. Then there were Nico, Benny, Willie and three fillies, little long-legged bundles of energy.

As they entered the stable Brother Bernard told Frans to make sure that he always let the ponies know where he was.

"Talk to them," he said, "so they get used to your voice. Never make unexpected moves but do touch them; they are sociable animals and they like contact. Don't ever be afraid of them, for they can sense if you are. If you are not afraid of them, they will not be afraid of you. First thing in the morning, let the ponies out in the small area outside the stable, clean out the stalls and put the dirty straw on the dung heap. Put fresh straw on the floor, and get clean drinking water from the faucet outside. Put hay in the hay rack, and four cups of oats in the feed buckets. Let the fillies in first while you brush the others outside. Then rake the area around the stable, but listen for the bell, because you have only ten minutes to get to class."

Back in class, some of the boys asked Frans where he had been and he proudly told them, "I am now in charge of the ponies."

"Do you really like it?" asked one of them. Frans only smiled.

Harry, one of the bigger kids said, "You smell like horse manure and are just a little farmer's boy." Frans wondered if Harry was jealous or if he was just plain nasty. Harry always hung out with a small group of loud bullies whom Frans did not like, and tried to stay away from them.

That night after dinner he wrote a letter to his parents. He told them all about the ponies, Brother Bernard, and how much he liked his new job, but forgot to ask his Mom if she could send him some old clothes.

Frans had to learn how to put bit and bridle on the ponies and tie them to a post before he could brush them, which was not easy as up close their heads were enormous. Brother Bernard stayed each morning for a little while until Frans was able to do it all by himself. One day Benny tried to bite Frans and kicked him in his leg. Luckily it did not hurt much. Slowly Frans gained the trust of his charges and he himself felt more and more comfortable with them. After that Brother Bernard still checked on Frans, but only now and then. Brother Bernard told Frans that he had made no mistake in selecting him as his helper. Frans glowed with pride.

Every morning after breakfast, then after lunch, and again after school from four until dinner time, Frans worked at the stables and enjoyed every minute of it. On Wednesday and Saturday afternoons, when there was no school, he did chores that took more time like cut grass and clean the equipment. Some days he delivered fruits and vegetables to the Pastor in town, something he liked to do because he loved to ride and be in charge of an important job.

Chapter 2
THE UNEXPECTED VISITOR

The war became more and more intense. The boys could hear planes from England fly over on their way to drop bombs on factories and cities in Germany. Often they listened to heavy gunfire and explosions. Lots of rumors were floating about. The local newspaper, which was controlled by the Germans, gave very little information. Frans knew about underground newspapers, which gave more factual news about the war, but he had never seen any. The brothers never expressed themselves about the war and the German occupation, but somehow the boys understood clearly where their loyalties were.

One evening, right after dinner, everybody, the brothers, the teachers, the boys and staff were told to go to the main assembly hall. As soon as everybody was seated, two German officers entered, and with the help of a translator, said that enemy airplanes had been shot down the day before and some airmen had parachuted out and escaped.

"Our soldiers are searching the whole area and if we find that any flyers are hiding here, we will close the school at once and all the brothers will be put in jail," they threatened. After repeating the threat and adding even more warnings, the officers left. Then Brother Superior spoke and said that all should be careful and to tell him if anyone saw anything suspicious.

The next day when Frans entered the stable, he noticed that the ponies were nervous. He checked them over, especially Willie, who lately had been behaving somewhat badly. He put her in a small separate corral behind the stable and planned to ask Brother Bernard that afternoon what else he should do. Frans stayed longer than usual brushing the ponies and talking to them, and was almost late for class. There all the boys were talking about what had happened the night before.

"Perhaps one of those planes was shot down not far from here," said one of Frans' classmates.

"Who knows, some of the pilots who parachuted out might be hiding somewhere nearby in the woods."

When Frans entered the stable after lunch, the ponies seemed to be even more agitated than they were in the morning. Then Frans heard a strange noise that seemed to come from the loft. Rats, Frans thought. . . rats were always a problem in a horse barn. He should find a way to get rid of them. Then he heard the noise again. This is not a rat, Frans thought. What else could it be?

He yelled, "Anybody up there?" This time he

heard what seemed to be a grunt. Frans moved the ladder that was standing against the wall and placed it so that he could climb up and look into the loft. Carefully he climbed the ladder, stuck his head slowly above the edge of the loft and froze. A man in uniform, clutching his side, was aiming a pistol right at him.

"*Nee, niet schieten.* (No, don't shoot). Please." "Please" was one of the few words Frans knew in English, along with "nice" and "thank you", which he repeated over and over. The man mumbled something and Frans seemed to hear the word "water" which is the same word in English and in Dutch. He quickly went down and got a cup of water and gave it to the stranger, and then got him another one. The man made a sign with his right hand like he was putting something into his mouth. Frans understood that the man was hungry. He nodded his head, descended the ladder, put it back and ran to find Brother Bernard to get some food. Suddenly he realized that he should not be running but should walk slowly so that nobody would become suspicious.

As soon as Frans found Brother Bernard, he told him, "Please come, something happened that I have to show you." Frans did not want to say what happened, because he was afraid they might be overheard. Back in the stable he put the ladder back in place, and told

Brother Bernard to go and see what was up there. The man had fallen asleep or was unconscious; he did not react even after Brother Bernard spoke to him in English. Brother Bernard descended the ladder, looked very seriously at Frans and said, "Nobody is to know about this, not even any of the other brothers, and that includes Brother Superior. You and I will have to take care of this man. He should not move from where he is, for the Germans are already suspicious. We will feed him and give him some of the blankets from the ponies. I think that he is not hurt too badly. When he is well, we will take action. This is our big secret, and ours alone."

Frans nodded; he understood the seriousness of the situation. That night, Frans barely slept, and at breakfast, did not even eat the two slices of bread that were allotted to each boy.

"Please, can I have that slice of bread?" begged one of his classmates.

"No," Frans told him, "I'll eat it later when I am finished with my work at the stable."

Brother Bernard was already at the stable when Frans arrived, and had also brought some bread and cheese from the rectory. As it turned out, the wounded man, whose name was Bill, was not badly hurt but he surely was hungry. He had parachuted out after his plane was shot down. He hid in the woods overnight and the next day when he saw the stable, he waited until evening to enter. Although the ponies almost panicked when he entered, he had been able to calm them down and climb into the loft.

"I hope my crew was able to get out also," Bill said. "When our plane was hit there was so much fire I couldn't see a thing." His main concern was that his parachute was still laying around somewhere, and should be hidden as soon as possible.

Brother Bernard asked Frans' teacher if he would excuse Frans from class for the morning. He told the teacher that one of the ponies was ill and that Frans was needed to help to take care of the animal. Frans wondered about Brother Bernard making up stories, actually lying. The brothers taught the boys to always tell the truth, and this was clearly a lie. Frans wondered, would lying be OK under special circumstances?

Instead of tending to the ponies Frans went looking for the parachute. Based on what Bill had told Brother Bernard, Frans should look at the edge of the forest, which he searched for quite some time. When he did not see anything there he started to look in the bushes, and finally found the parachute. At first he wanted to bring it to the stable, but then he thought, "What if somebody comes by here? They might see it." So instead Frans got a shovel, dug a hole in the side of a ditch, put the parachute in it and made sure that it was well hidden under dirt and leaves. He was sweating when he came back to the stable, where Brother Bernard was anxiously waiting for him.

"Well done," Brother Bernard said, "we can always go back later and retrieve it." Back in the recreation hall that evening, Frans told some of the boys that one of the ponies was ill and that he might have to stay with her again.

"Now you are also a veterinarian?" sneered Harry. Frans acted as if he did not hear him.

Chapter 3
HIDING

Frans took an instant liking to Bill. He felt sorry for him and admired his good spirits. Bill was American, born on a farm near Crowley, a small town in Louisiana. His ancestry was partly Austrian. German had been the language of his grandparents. Consequently, Bill spoke German, which made it easier for Frans and Bill to understand each other because the German language is closer to Dutch than English, and many words sound alike. Growing up, Bill had worked on his father's farm, but as soon as he could, joined the Air Force as he was fascinated with flying. Bill married a local girl, Celestine, a descendent of the Acadians who in the 18th Century were forced out of Canada and relocated to the bayous of southern Louisiana. The couple had two children: Marie, the oldest and Mickey, who had just turned 11. Bill was terribly worried about his family, who would not know whether he was alive or dead.

"I'll see if one of my friends can help out," Brother Bernard said. "I know there are groups that help downed pilots and people that are hiding from the Germans. Perhaps they might be able to get word to

Bill's family, and let them know that Bill is alive and well. Who knows, they might also help Bill get back to England," he added. A few days later, somebody who was in contact with a local group of the Resistance told Brother Bernard that they would certainly try to take care of Bill. The Resistance had been able to smuggle airmen back to England by way of France and Spain and would also like to help Bill get back home. They suggested that Bill should stay a while longer where he was, for the Germans, knowing that airmen had escaped, were especially vigilant. In the mean time plans would be made to get Bill off the grounds of the boarding school and to a safe place to prepare him for what would be a very dangerous trip. The Resistance would provide Bill with fake identification, Dutch money and addresses to stay at while en route.

That evening at dinner time, Harry started to yell at Frans. "Man, you must be crazy. We all know you are talking to the ponies, but are you trying to teach them German? They should send you to the nuthouse. I heard you when I was near the stable this afternoon. What are you doing there all the time anyway?"

"I was practicing for my language class," Frans said. That night Frans dreamed of being picked up by Germans, Bill being dragged away, and Brother Bernard being beaten.

The next morning Brother Bernard, Bill and Frans had a serious discussion. Something had to be done, and soon. Bill had to leave, but how?

Chapter 4
ON THE RUN

"If we just knew a place where Bill could hide," Frans said. "I could take him there. We could use the pony cart and hide Bill underneath some fruits and vegetables. I could pretend that I make a delivery in the village." The brothers, knowing how bad things were in the village, had occasionally brought surplus fruit and vegetables from their farm to the Pastor of the church, to be distributed to those most in need. With no gasoline available, the pony cart was used to transport the food. In the beginning the Germans often checked the contents of the cart, but after some time they got used to seeing Frans, and no longer paid any attention.

Brother Bernard decided to go to the village and pay a courtesy visit to the Pastor. He knew the Pastor, but not really well enough to be sure he was not pro-German. He had to play his cards carefully. The Pastor soon understood what was expected from him and told Brother Bernard that Bill could hide in his church, at least untill the Resistance would be able to take care of him.

"How tall is Bill and what size shoes does he

wear?" the Pastor asked. "I'll get some civilian clothes for him from one of my parishioners." The Resistance was informed and arrangements were made to take Bill the following Saturday afternoon to the church. Frans would take care of the transportation of this very special load. That day it rained and although Frans disliked driving in the rain, this Saturday he welcomed the raindrops dancing on the pavement. Moreover, it was not at all suspicious to have a tarp over the food. Brother Bernard considered it a good omen. As nervous as he was, Frans tried to stay calm.

Just out of the gate a German soldier came up to him and asked, "What do you have in that cart?"

"I am taking fruits and vegetables to the church," Frans said. "We do that all the time," he added.

The soldier lifted up the tarp, took one of the apples, and said, "Keep going."

Arriving at the church, the Pastor told Frans to drive around the back to the door near the cemetery.

As soon as they had started to unload the cart, a man who was working nearby came and said, "Let me help you."

The Pastor told him, "Thanks for the offer, but we can do this by ourselves. Please go on."

The man insisted, "I want to help." Then suddenly he yelled, "You are hiding something! You are hiding a man, I am going to tell!" and ran away.

The Pastor pulled the last few boxes from the cart and said, "Both of you, run, go, leave now! Here are the clothes I got for you. Change somewhere and hide your uniform, but both of you have to leave now. I will deal with the Germans, when they come. As a priest, I. . ." Bill and Frans did not hear anything more, as they were already running, running across the cemetery, jumping over the wall towards the fields beyond the village. When they saw a ditch they dove into it. Frans was exhausted and so was Bill. It was late afternoon, but still hours before dark.

"Let's rest a while and think about what we can do; undoubtedly the Germans will start looking for us. We will need to find a place for the night. There are some farms nearby but how do we know who we can trust?" Frans knew that the Dutch cherished their independence, but as in any society some people sided with the enemy and took advantage of the occupation. Moreover, the Germans offered rewards, especially for an American pilot!

"Let's stay here and pull some reeds over us," Frans suggested.

A group of men came out of the village, spread out and started walking through the fields. Two of them were soldiers carrying rifles. The other men, probably farmers who were forced to help find the escapees. Bill and Frans pressed themselves deeper against the ground, afraid to look up. One of the men passed within a few feet of them.

Bill held his breath, and he cocked his pistol. Although the man must have seen them, he kept on walking without changing his pace. Both Bill and Frans sighed a sigh of relief. Frans realized that there were still some good Dutchmen. It gave hope that maybe, maybe, things would work out.

They waited until it started to get dark before they got on hands and knees to survey the surroundings. A short distance to the east was a farm with barns for livestock and equipment. They needed to find a roof over their heads. Although it was spring, the nights were still cold. Whatever they had to do, it would be risky. When it was completely dark they got up. A watery moon provided an eerie light. As they were getting near the buildings, a dog barked, and the pair froze. They heard a man's voice tell the dog to keep quiet. When they got closer, the dog barked again and the man came outside.

"Quiet, Bruno, quiet!" The man looked around and told the dog again to stop barking, and took him inside. After that, everything remained silent. Frans and Bill crept to the building farthest away from the main house and searched for a door. Quietly they went inside.

The following morning, Frans slipped out early and went to the road. From there he approached the farm and knocked on the door. He told the farmer that he came from a town nearby, asking for food. Then he started to tell the farmer and his wife that he had somebody with him who had to stay out of sight.

It was as if the woman sensed what was happening, and she asked, "Where is he? We will help anyone who comes to help us." Together they went to the barn. "Stay here, both of you," the woman said, "I will bring water, soap, towels and food. We will decide later on what we will do next."

The farmer told Bill that he could stay and gave him work clothes."You can work together with the other farmhands," the farmer said, "and if anybody talks to you just answer in German, or even better, let others do the talking."

Frans was very worried about his parents. By now they must have heard that he had run away and surely would be very anxious. Frans wrote them a short note:

> *I am OK. I will contact you again,*
> *I love you very much,*
> *Frans.*

One of the farmhands on his way home that evening would put the letter in the mailbox at the post office. Frans could not tell his parents where he was because he was afraid that the letter might be intercepted.

Chapter 5
CAUGHT

America, Britain and the other Allied nations were preparing to attack the German forces from the sea. Their air forces had been bombing the cities and factories in Germany to do as much damage to the German war machine as possible. The invasion of Europe was imminent. Then, on June 6, 1944, it finally happened.

It took a few days before the news reached Bill and Frans. Nothing changed, but somehow one could feel that liberation was in the air. The German occupiers became frantic and their behavior more and more irrational. Most nights the sky was lit up by searchlights and explosions, but the American and British planes kept coming. When a plane crashed just a few miles from the farm, Bill became distraught and wanted to go and help his comrades.

"Stay here, Bill! Don't go. You will be caught." Frans said.

"But I want to do something," Bill answered. "I don't want to hide any longer. I want to get back to my squadron, and help bring this war to an end. It seems as if there are now more German troops around, and the risk of being discovered is growing by the day."

"I'll go with you," Frans insisted. "Staying here is as dangerous for me as it is for you. Besides, I speak Dutch and know the countryside."

Bill and Frans got some maps of the surrounding area. To go south they had to cross a river but could not use the bridge or a ferry because the Germans always checked for identification papers at those places.

"If we can't find a boat we will just have to swim across," Frans said, "I can swim real well and that river is not very wide. I have won a number of trophies for our swim team," he added, trying to convince Bill. They decided not to tell the farmer or anybody else, because they might try to talk them out of it. Their plan was to go for a walk one afternoon and then not return to the farm. That way they would already be closer to the river before nightfall. Moreover, if they hid a backpack with clothes, a flashlight and some food, they could pick it up on the way. It all was very risky but they saw no other way.

A drizzle hung over men and meadows as they went on their way. They had walked only a mile or so when they saw a group of people coming towards them. Friends or foe? They could not tell. Frans grasped Bill's hand.

"Keep walking and act as if nothing is happening," Bill said. The group passed; they were German soldiers, who paid no attention to them.

When twilight fell over the fields they looked for a place to hide until dark.

"We have to be careful, we have to reach the river in time, so we can get across before daylight. I don't want to provide target practice for our German friends," Bill said sarcastically.

On the horizon searchlights crisscrossed the sky, and flashing tracers pierced the low-hanging clouds. Explosions reverberated over the drone of aircraft engines. High overhead it was like a Chinese New Year gone berserk; down below an eerie silence reigned.

It was nearly midnight when they got to the river's edge. They saw a large tree limb, which they dragged into the water to help them float. Bill took a rope, fastened it to Frans' belt and then onto himself. For a moment they held each other tight.

Only once they started to float Bill whispered, "Good luck. Let the current do most of the work. The less movement and noise we make, the better the chance that we will not get noticed. The map shows that the next village is miles away. We can easily get across before there."

"As long as I can see Bill, I will be OK," Frans

thought. The water was cold, and the current stronger than they expected. They tried not to make a sound. When they got close to the other shore they heard the sound of a motor. They paddled ever so softly and hid under some weeping willows that crowded the water's edge. The motor droned on, but did not seem to come closer nor go further away. Then there was the sound of footsteps and muffled voices. Were they Germans? A security detail patrolling the river? The cold water started to have an effect on Frans. He thought that he would lose consciousness, which he might have, for suddenly he felt something on his arm.

It was Bill, who whispered, "Keep your head down and slowly climb ashore, but stay down." Carefully, he took off Frans' jacket and shirt and rubbed his body with a wool shirt which he took out of the backpack. Through his half-opened eyes Frans could see a shimmering of light. Frans felt cold and miserable. He wished he would be anywhere but here, if he just could be with his Mom and Dad, his friends at home or even at the boarding school. Frans remembered how happy he had been taking care of the ponies. They were like friends, real friends. Frans needed desperately to hold onto something. Never in his life had he felt so lonely. He grabbed Bill's hand. Bill put his arm around Frans' shoulder and held him tight.

Then Bill said, "You don't know, Frans, how sorry I am to have gotten you into this mess. You saved my life, and I can never do enough to repay you. We will get through this together. We have to. When all this is over you'll have to come to America. I want you to meet my family. Please promise me that you will."

They stayed against the summer dike, which is the bank of the actual river. Further inland was the main dike which protects the countryside during early spring, when the water is high from the rains and melting snow from the mountains in Germany. The Dutch know that this wide stretch of land, the flood plain, gives the river the space it needs during times of high water, and protects the fields and villages. The road on the top of the winter dike carries a lot of traffic. Since there are no buildings on the flood plain, which is used only for grazing cattle and sheep, two people crossing the plain in daylight would easily be noticed. Bill felt Frans' forehead and knew Frans had a fever, and said, "Try and sleep, I'll be the lookout." Time went by slowly. At nightfall they finally dared to advance to the main dike.

Just as Bill, who went first, tried to cross the dike, a voice rang out. "*Halt! Wer ist da?*" (Stop! Who is there?)

Bill answered in German, "I was checking on my

cow who is giving birth any day now." But the soldier did not want to believe him.

"It is past curfew, you can't be out after dark. March! To the commandant." Then the German soldier saw Frans. "Get lost, boy," he said, "or do you want me to take you too?" Frans ran towards a row of houses built against the dike. He looked back only to see Bill, with the soldier's gun in his back, walking the other way. The first door he saw he knocked on. The man who opened the door looked scared. When he saw it was only a boy, he quickly pulled him inside. Frans blurted out the whole story. He felt sick, miserable and ready to die at any moment. The lady of the house gave him something warm to drink and some medicine and put him to bed. "Sleep, my boy," she said, " you are in good hands."

In the mean time, Bill had followed the soldier's order and moved slowly forward. Then he bent over and reached for his shoe.

The soldier asked "What are you doing?"

Bill replied, "Tying my shoelace." The soldier let the butt of his gun rest on the ground. Bill grabbed it and with one sweep hit the soldier on the side of his head. The blow was so quick and unexpected that the soldier fell to the ground. Bill laid right next to him and waited a few moments. Everything remained quiet. He pulled the man off the roadway and placed him under some bushes. Bill didn't think he had killed the man, who actually looked more like a boy.

"Lucky for me," Bill thought. "If he had been an experienced soldier, I would now be somewhere I don't want to be." Bill realized he now had two challenges: to stay out of the hands of the Germans, and to find Frans.

Chapter 6
RESISTANCE

When Frans woke up the following morning he had a long talk with the lady of the house, Mrs. De Vries. Her husband, a teacher, had left for school. She said that Frans could stay until he felt better and suggested they try to contact his parents. This would have to be done carefully, because the Germans must now also be looking for Frans as a way to find Bill.

When Mr. De Vries came home that evening, he said that rumors were abound. "Last night somebody beat up a young German soldier on the dike and put him under some shrubbery. The soldier reported taking a man with a funny German accent in custody for breaking curfew when the prisoner attacked him. He also remembered that there was a young boy nearby but wasn't sure if the two were together."

Mr. De Vries resolved that it would be prudent for Frans to stay out of sight, at least for a little while. In the mean time he would try to find a way to get a message to Frans' parents so they at least would know that he was OK.

Frans was anxious, for he had not heard from his parents for weeks. He was even more worried about

Bill who, although he apparently had escaped; he was now surely being hunted by the Germans. Frans could not stop thinking about Bill, who had become such a good friend, and someone he admired and loved.

Bill remained in the neighborhood. He felt somehow responsible for Frans, although logic would tell him that Frans would be better off without him. Frans was Dutch and more likely to find people who would take care of him. He would, or at least should, be able to find his parents and even go back to the boarding school. It was he, Bill, who had caused all the trouble. Still he felt it was his duty to at least make sure that Frans was all right.

Bill's most urgent problem was food, because, even if he had money, he had no ration coupons. Small groups of people, old folks, parents with children, some pulling baby carriages, others with bikes with wooden tires, were going from farm to farm begging for food. Bill pulled his cap low over his forehead, pretended to be lame in one leg and joined one of these desperate groups. He did not say a word, and no one paid any attention to him. When arriving at a farmhouse the door would open and sometimes the farmer would say he had no more food. Other times some bread or other food would be placed in the outstretched hands. Seeing how hungry all of the city people were, Bill was embarrassed to take food that otherwise would have gone to a famished woman or child. Bill had never begged in his life and felt uncomfortable doing so. He reluctantly put out his hand, touched by all the suffering he saw around him.

One farmer pointed at Bill and said, "I need some help, please come with me." Bill understood what he meant and went inside. At first, Bill acted like he was deaf, but the farmer seemed like a good sort of fellow and Bill confessed that he needed help.

"I thought so," said the farmer, who spoke enough English to understand Bill. "I figured you might be the guy who beat up that damn German. That's why I picked you out. Hide in the back kitchen, have something to eat and be patient. I have friends who help people like you."

Bill could not believe his luck. The farmer told Bill that he could stay, at least for a few days. That night he slept in a cow stable but didn't mind the smell at all.

When he came home the following evening, Mr. De Vries told Frans that he heard from "friends" that Bill was OK. He even knew where Bill was hiding and could bring Frans there. It was better that Frans would leave his house anyway because his next door neighbor was a member of the NSB, the Dutch National Socialist Party, a most despised organization. Its members collaborated with the German occupiers.

It was after midnight when they left and went to the farm where Bill was anxiously waiting for Frans, who was overjoyed to see him. They hugged each other.

"How did you get away?" Frans asked. "Never in my life have I been so worried."

Bill told Frans in detail what had happened to him and how he was able to escape after he was caught on the dike.

The farmer, who wanted to be known as Mr. 'K', told Frans that he knew an address in town where Frans would be welcome. "Tomorrow morning I will bring you there. In the mean time, would you be willing to help us?" he added.

"Of course I will," Frans said.

"But this is no farm work," the farmer said. Frans was secretly relieved. He did not like such work, unless he could take care of horses.

"Information," Mr. 'K', explained to Frans, "is of the greatest importance. Keeping people informed of what really is going on. The newspapers only print what the Germans allow them to print. We have an underground press and need people to distribute the papers. It is risky: if you get caught, it is unlikely we can help you." Frans thought of Bill, who came from a foreign country, risking his life for people he didn't even know.

Mr. 'K' continued, "Bill will also be working

with us. He has knowledge and skills we badly need. It is unlikely that you will see him for quite some time, but we all hope that when this awful war is over you will meet again."

Frans and Bill talked through the night. It seemed like a lifetime ago when they had first met, and yet these last few weeks had gone by so fast. Frans realized that he tried to hold on to the past, but now the past was gone. From now on he would have to stand on his own two feet, and make his own decisions. He now knew what it really meant to be all alone. No one, not even Bill, could help him.

The next morning Mr. 'K' brought Frans to his new home. On the way Mr. 'K' explained what the work entailed. "We will contact you by phone or messenger and tell you where to pick up and drop off the papers. The newspapers will be hidden in rolls of packing paper or boxes with food or other merchandise. A code will be used that only you will know. The first packages will not contain any newspapers to make sure that if the Germans stop you they will not find anything. I am not going to tell you when you are transporting newspapers, so be careful from the very beginning."

Chapter 7
A NEW FAMILY

And so Frans started a new life as the "grandson" of Mr. and Mrs. van Houten. Both of them were in their late sixties and retired. They lived on the edge of town, in a red-tiled cottage, surrounded by blooming rhododendrons and towering gladiolas. They could have been his grandparents, and asked Frans to call them Opa and Oma, which is Dutch for Grandfather and Grandmother. They indeed, treated him as family. He got his own bedroom and they shared all they had with him.

As in all households in occupied Holland, food was in short supply. Breakfast was one slice of bread, with only once in a while some cheese or jam. The other meals consisted of soup, made from potatoes or cabbage or some boiled macaroni, usually without any cheese. Fish and meat were rare. The fruit trees in the garden provided anjou pears and golden delicious apples, which were indeed delicious and a welcome addition to their diet.

Mr. van Houten had for many years, and with great pride and determination, bred Barnefelders and Dutch Bantam chickens and looked upon them as one of his greatest accomplishments. It was with great reluctance that he had allowed them to become part of an ever-more scarce diet. When only two of his priced specimens were left, the ones which he had planned to save as a special treat for Christmas, he became so upset over all the ruthless and needless killings going on everywhere that he could no longer stomach the idea of slaughtering them. He gave them away to strangers. Frans understood and agreed with his Opa that the need for food did not justify killing something that was so dear to him. Frans was also secretly relieved, for he did not relish the prospect of eating those beautiful animals. Frans hoped that he would never be so hungry that he even would consider doing so.

Frans never complained, for his hosts were sharing their food ration coupons with him. He told them once how sorry he felt for them, but they forbade him to ever mention it again.

Mr. van Houten was a great storyteller and in the evenings talked about the many things he had experienced in his long life. Frans learned a lot about the war.

Mr. van Houten explained. "The great war of 1914-18 had turned out badly for the Germans. The conditions of the peace treaty of Versailles were very severe. Germany lost parts of its territory, and had to pay an enormous amount of money as reparation. With the infrastructure in ruin, the country sunk into a deep depression. Inflation was rampant." Mr. van Houten showed Frans some postage stamps from Germany from the 1920's. "Look," he said, "the denominations are for 500,000 and 1,000,000 Marks, which at one time were equal to the Dutch Guilder. Inflation became so bad that the price of bread rose daily. Food and basic necessities became too expensive for people, especially for pensioners and others living on a fixed income. Many people lost their life savings almost overnight. Riots broke out everywhere. Germany became ungovernable. Adolf Hitler, an Austrian, became leader of the rightist Nazi party and promised to bring the country back to stability, wealth and power. Most people were so desperate they were willing to believe anyone. In 1933 Hitler was elected Reichkanseler or Prime Minister. From then on he had a free hand. He believed that the German race was superior and should conquer the world. He wanted to destroy all other races. In 1938 he annexed Austria and in September 1939 invaded Poland."

"But why did he attack Holland?" Frans asked. "Holland stayed neutral in the first World War," Frans remembered from his history class.

"Hitler needed access to the North Sea," Mr. van

Houten answered, "for one of his main goals was to conquer England."

"But nobody tried to stop him?" Frans asked incredulously.

"Yes, many did, but Hitler, through his special troops, the SS, instilled fear in everyone. It was a dangerous time for the Germans. Opposing the regime meant concentration camp or death." Frans realized that even if he could do little, he wanted to help to bring this ordeal to an end.

Within a few days his orders to deliver the newspapers came in. Sometimes he would find a package behind a garbage can in an alley, then under some bushes or behind one of the low walls that surround many Dutch gardens. Frans brought the underground newspapers to different addresses in the area. The papers, which consisted of one or two sheets of mimeographed paper, were in blank envelopes and Frans would slip most of them in mail slots. At other places he brought them inside, such as at the butcher's shop, but only when no customers were present.

One day, while delivering at one of the farms, he saw a girl his own age slip away from the farmyard. He called after her and asked her for her name.

"I am Sarah," the girl answered. She seemed very nervous and said, "Nobody knows I am here. Please don't tell anybody you saw me."

"Of course I will not tell anybody, why should I do that?" Frans said, "I work for the Resistance." The lady of the house came into the farmyard and asked them to come in the kitchen. There she told Frans to be sure to keep it a secret that he had seen Sarah. Frans and Sarah talked for a long time, happy to have met someone their own age with whom they could spend some time.

Frans told Sarah what had happened to him and asked, "But why are you here? You have not done anything illegal, have you?"

"No, but my family is Jewish and the Germans hate us and want to send us to concentration camps. Soon after the Germans occupied Holland they started to make life difficult for us. We had to wear the yellow Star of David on our clothes, and could not use public transportation like the streetcars and buses any more. My father, who was a teacher at a high school, was fired because he was Jewish. In May, 1942 he was arrested and sent to a concentration camp in Germany. We have never heard from him again and don't even know whether he is alive or dead." Sarah's dark amber eyes filled with tears. Frans held her hand but did not know what to say.

Sarah continued, "My mom and I hid for a long time in the attic of a friend's home in Amsterdam, but when the people who were hiding us could not provide us with food any longer, we had to leave. You see, we don't get any ration coupons for food or clothing and my mom ran out of money to buy them on the black market. Somebody knew Mr. and Mrs. Renselaar and they let me stay with them. My mother is at another farm, but I don't even know where that is. We are afraid that if either of us is caught we might betray the other."

Chapter 8
A MOST SUSPICIOUS FIRE

"We need some extra people to serve as lookouts in a few days. Can we count on you?" Mr. 'K' asked Frans. "Can you be there on Friday night at 11 o'clock near the place where Bill beat the German soldier? A man who calls himself Geert will take you to where you have to be. Mr. van Houten will not ask any questions." That Friday night there was a heavy fog and Frans almost missed his contact, but Geert saw the boy first. Together they walked silently across the flood plain.

"Stay here," Geert said and handed Frans a flashlight. "Watch both directions of the dike. If you see anything suspicious, like a group of cars or trucks, or motorcycles, point the flashlight in the direction of the river, and flick the light twice. You stay down. We expect a munitions drop. If you see two short flashes coming from the river, leave right away. Good luck."

Frans felt scared. There were many sounds in the night he could not place. An hour passed. The fog turned into a drizzle. He told himself that he had to be brave: people depended on him, and he was now part of a bigger operation. Frans was proud that he was asked to help.

The wind picked up and the wet leaves on the trees made a swishing sound. A dog barked in the distance. An automobile, with dim lights drove slowly by on the dike road. Germans searching for something, Frans wondered?.

"Watch out! Can't you see where you're going?" The low German voice sounded angry. Frans dropped to the ground. The sound came from less than thirty meters away. Frans lifted his head up ever so slightly. He saw four shadows crouching, and heard the click-clacking of rifle bolts being cocked. How was it possible that he had not heard them coming? Too late to use the flashlight now!

Frans waited a few, interminable minutes, then started to creep toward the large dike and the roadway. All kinds of thoughts raced through his mind. "I'll have to draw their attention from the munitions drop," he told himself. As he got close to the dike Frans turned on the flashlight, sprang up, ran across the roadway while letting out a loud scream. Shots rang out as he dove into the wet grass on the other side of the dike. Frans was lucky the grass was tall because the sheep who normally grazed there, and had kept the grass short, had been taken to Germany months before. He crawled until he came to an orchard at the bottom of the dike, and then ran in the opposite direction from his home.

Whatever happens, he thought, the Germans must not find out where Opa and Oma live. He slipped into a backyard and hid behind a shed. There he waited for what seemed an eternity. Frans knew the area pretty well and was able to get to his home undetected.

The moment he opened the backdoor he saw his Opa sitting in the dark waiting for him. Frans threw his arms around his Opa and started to cry.

'I'm so scared Opa, I'm so scared."

"It is OK now, you are safe now,"comforted Opa. "I'll get you something to drink and you can tell me what happened."

Frans told Opa the story with all of the details.

Holland is a very organized country. Perhaps because it is the most densely populated country in the western world everything is subject to rules. There a an old saying: "The Dutch rule the water, but the rules rule the Dutch." The public registry contains all information about everybody. Obviously the Germans made good use of that to round up people. Many had to leave their homes and hide wherever they could. The Resistance decided that something had to be done about this. In most cities, those registry offices were located in the town hall. Quite a few suddenly and mysteriously burned down, destroying a lot of vital statistics. The fire department often showed up a little late and used much more water than was really necessary, causing even more damage. Now each town hall was well guarded by armed German soldiers.

Mr. 'K' told Frans that his organization wanted to destroy the town hall in a nearby town. They were planning to burn down the building. It would help if there were flammable materials inside to feed the fire once it started. Could Frans help?

The following Thursday morning Frans rode his bike to Vossendam. The town hall, a late Gothic building, stood in the center of town. Frans put his bike in the bicycle stand, ran up the flight of stairs and entered through the large wooden doors.

The receptionist smiled at Frans and said, "Sorry, young man, you are in the wrong office. Besides, tell you Mom or Dad to come themselves, for they will not give food ration coupons to kids."

"Where is the bathroom?" asked Frans, "I really need to go." She pointed him in the right direction. Frans quickly went inside and hid a parcel in the back of the toilet. On Friday, he went back to the town hall late in the afternoon, hoping that somebody else would be at the counter and that he would not be recognized. Luckily, this time there was a man. After again asking the way to the bathroom, Frans walked around a bit until he saw a garbage can. He dropped the package into the can. Since the town hall was open on Saturday morning from nine until noon, Mr. 'K' asked Frans to go yet again.

Just as he entered the front door one of the soldiers standing guard called out, "Hey, you, stop. Why are you here again? Do you have to be here every day?"

"I have to give this package to my mother, who works here," Frans said.

"Go, but come right back, or else." The soldier looked at his watch. Frans ran inside. He went up the stairs, looked for a door that said "Janitor-Do Not Enter," went inside and poured gasoline behind some boxes. He ran out and thanked the soldier in his best German.

On Monday the local newspaper ran a front page article. "Town Hall Burns to the Ground. Suspicious Fire Destroys Building. Fire Department Unable to Save Any of the Records."

Frans did not want the other children in the neighborhood to get to know him too well because he was afraid they would ask too many questions. Instead he stayed home with Oma, and helped her in the vegetable garden. She in turn helped Frans learn English. Mrs. van Houten had been a teacher and

Frans proved to be an excellent student, and soon they were having entire conversations in English.

"I am doing this for Bill," Frans thought. "Won't Bill be surprised and happy not to have to speak German with me any more." The thought of Bill always made Frans feel uneasy. Knowing that Bill would be doing whatever the Resistance asked of him, Frans had no doubt that Bill would take risks to help free Holland from the Germans.

After making some deliveries of underground newspapers, Frans came home one afternoon and put his bike in the chicken coop. Since the chickens were gone, it was now used to store the bikes and garden tools.

As soon as he opened the back door, he heard people talking in the hall. The sound of a German voice scared Frans. He was struck with fright. He asked himself, "Did the Germans find out that I deliver underground papers?" Drops of perspiration formed on his forehead. His hands felt clammy.

Before he could turn around, the voice of Mr. van Houten called out, "Is that you, Frans?" Mr. van Houten opened the door to the kitchen and gestured at Frans to come closer.

"Come here boy, let me introduce you to Sergeant Klaussen." Frans came slowly forward and saw a tall German soldier with friendly blue eyes that smiled at him from behind rimless eyeglasses.

Shaking Frans' hand he asked in broken Dutch, "How are you young man? Having fun playing outside?"

"I was riding my bike. Just riding around. Not doing anything in particular. Just riding around," Frans stammered. Sergeant Klaussen turned towards Mr. van Houten.

"Please allow me to come back in a few days to see how your wife is coming along. I am really concerned and wish you and her the very best." Without waiting for an answer, he turned towards Frans and said, "You, young man, take good care of your grandparents." He saluted and left through the front door.

Frans turned to his Opa, "What happened? Did he find out about the newspapers?" Frans asked.

"I don't know what you are talking about. In any case, don't ever talk about those things. They are none of anybody's business," Opa said. "No, he came here because of Oma. Sergeant Klaussen was in the sidecar of a motorcycle when the driver, being careless, almost hit Oma as she was crossing the street. She fell and hurt her hip and scraped both her knees. He sent someone to get a doctor and ask him to come here as soon as possible. In the mean time he brought Oma home and took very good care of her. It seems he was really concerned." Frans ran into the living room where Mrs. van Houten was sitting on the couch with towels covering her legs.

"Oma, Oma, are you OK?" Frans asked as he hugged her. Just then the doorbell rang and the doctor entered. Frans left the room and went to his bedroom. I have to be more careful, he said to himself. I am sure Opa knows what I am doing but I promised never, ever to mention it to anybody that I help the Resistance, and today I did it twice. I have to act more grown up. After all, I am already twelve years old.

Two days later Sergeant Klaussen came to see Mrs. van Houten again. He not only brought a bouquet of flowers, but also a loaf of bread, some ham, a sausage and two bars of soap. Oma thought it was especially thoughtful of a man to think of bringing soap, an item that had disappeared from store shelves a long time ago.

"Don't mention it to anyone," Sergeant Klaussen said, "but I am sure you can use it. Your grandson, what is his name again? He is at the age that he needs to eat well, and I know that can be a problem in these difficult times." Just then Frans entered. Sergeant Klaussen asked Frans about his school. Frans answered in German that for some time now there had been no classes. "You speak German very well," Sergeant Klaussen remarked, "You must be a very good student." Luckily for Frans Mrs. van Houten answered, bragging about how smart Frans was. Frans excused himself and left. It was confusing to be talking to a man who was so nice but at the same time was also an enemy.

Chapter 9
SINT NICOLAAS

After the Allies landed on the beaches of Normandy, they liberated France, crossed into Belgium, and fought their way north to the border of Holland. To maintain this momentum, and to extricate the enemy from the Netherlands, the Allied forces planned one of the most daring operations of the war. "Operation Market Garden", the largest airborne offensive ever undertaken. The goal was to get control of all the bridges in eastern Holland and to open the roads to the center of the country.

On the sunny Sunday of September 17, 1944, the skies over southern Holland hummed with the sound of countless airplanes. Parachutes by the thousands floated down from the heavens like colorful confetti on an ecstatic population who anticipated freedom.

But freedom had not yet come.

Despite the heroic efforts of the thousands of paratroopers who jumped north of Arnhem, despite the hundreds of gliders that landed alongside of them, and despite the untold lives that were lost in the fierce fighting that followed, the Allied troops were unable to gain control of the bridge over the Rhine River at

Arnhem, which forever since has been referred to as "The Bridge Too Far."

Frans watched the glow of the battles in the southern sky at night which, as it turned out, was not the fulfilment of the dream that the war soon would be over. The illumination was not the dawn of freedom. To the contrary, in the days that followed the roads northwards were filled with sad-looking Dutch refugees burdened by what few possessions they managed to save.

Unable to cross the Rhine in Holland, the Allied High Command decided to push eastwards into Germany. The southern part of Holland was freed but the provinces above the Rhine River remained in German hands. For the people living there the worst part of the war was still to come. Frans felt as if a large gate closed in front of him. Although he was only thirty miles away from his parents, they might as well have been on another continent. Their city, Nijmegen, was liberated: he was still living under the German yoke.

Winter came early, and turned out to be the coldest of the century. By early November it was already freezing at night. Coal, which was used for generating electricity and for heating homes and factories, came from the mines in Limburg in the far south of Holland. But, because of the war, there were no shipments of any sort from the liberated parts of the free part of the country to the German-held provinces north of the Rhine. Because of the lack of electricity, most factories and businesses were closed, and so were the schools.

With all this misery going on there was, at least for the children, one bright point: Soon it would be December 6, the birthday of Sint Nicholaas, the greatest friend of all the children in Holland. Frans, remembered how excited he used to be as a young child to receive all those gifts from this Holy Bishop from Spain, who for centuries had come to Holland at the end of each November, to give gifts to all the children who had been good, and punish those who had been bad. Seeing the pictures in the newspaper of Sint Nicolaas, with his white horse "*Schimmel*"and helpers "*Zwarte Pieten*" arriving by boat in Amsterdam harbor, and greeted by the mayor and city officials, Frans always wondered if he had behaved as well as he knew he should have. For weeks prior to Sint Nicolaas' day he had put a shoe filled with a carrot in front of the chimney for "Schimmel," and sang as loud as he could the traditional songs. What a surprise and pleasure it had been, every year to find on the diningroom table the gifts he had hoped for. Only when he was a bit older, he wondered how in one night Sint Nicolaas could ride on his horse over all the rooftops and drop gifts through all those chimneys.

From then on, Frans participated in "*pakjes avond*" (gift giving evening) with his parents, family and friends. Frans remembered it as being the most exciting evening of the year, because the exchange of gifts was always accompanied by poems and surprises, which gave him a chance to even tease his own parents.

This year, perhaps because of the war, nobody had seen Sint Nicolaas arrive.

The children still sang the well-known songs at night before they went to bed, still set out their shoe, this year replacing the traditional carrot with some grass or hay for the horse, and still hoped that on December 6 their place at the table would be filled with gifts brought by the Holy Bishop from Spain.

Frans knew that he should not expect much. He decided to surprise his grandparents by making some gifts for them, which would show his love and appreciation toward them.

In his school's art class he had learned how to make puppets. He collected paper, pieces of cloth, wire, and from what little money he had, bought starch, brushes and paint. It was hard work, with much improvising, but he constructed a doll with a real likeness of Oma. He spent even more time creating a poem which customarily has to accompany each gift, and placed it in the arms of the doll.

> *On this special day in December*
> *It is good that I should remember*
> *That of all the gifts I get all year*
> *None of them can be so dear*
> *As the love and care I get each day*
> *I love you Oma is all that I can say.*
> *Your grandson Frans.*

For Opa Frans carved a walking stick from a branch of a tree, and in the poem for his Opa he teased him, in a typical Dutch way, that years from now, this cane might come in handy.

Frans' grandparents had not forgotten Sint Nicolaas either. Oma presented Frans with a woolen scarf and gloves that she had knitted herself, by unraveling one of Opa's old sweaters and reusing the yarn. From Opa Frans got a pocket knife, a happy surprise, for which he was very thankful. Together they sang-old-time Sint Nicolaas songs and played board games all evening long.

As Christmas came closer Frans thought more and more about his parents. He missed them so much. Never had he been away from home so long, Not knowing how his parents were doing was the worst part. He longed to be able to talk to them, if only for a few minutes. He hated the war.

His grandparents tried to make him feel better. Although Frans realized that he was lucky to be loved by them, he really missed his Mom and Dad.

Frans hoped that the New Year would bring him and his parents together, but all the New Year brought was more misery. Food became even more scarce; the store shelves stayed empty. Even with ration coupons there was little anybody could buy.

The previous September, the Dutch government-in-exile in London, hoping that Operation Market Garden would be successful, had called for the Dutch railway workers to go on strike. A general strike ensued but the Germans reacted swiftly, and took over the railroads. An unintended consequence of the strike was that the transportation of food by rail came to a complete stop. With all canals and waterways frozen solid, the movement of goods by boat, which was still a common form of transportation, had stopped also. The scarcity of food was now extreme.

People trekked into the countryside in search for anything to eat. Because of the lack of money, valuables like rings, brooches, fine linens, and even furniture, often heirlooms, were traded for potatoes, flour, fruit or anything edible. It took several days, on foot or by bike from the big cities like Amsterdam and

Den Haag, to reach villages and farms where there was still some food available. The city people were grateful to be allowed to stay overnight in a pigsty, sleeping on straw under blankets they had carried with them. Frans wanted to go also, to collect food for his grandparents, but they didn't want to hear of it.

"We would rather be hungry, for at least we are together. Moreover it is too dangerous," Mr. van Houten said. "Among all those poor people on the roads there are thieves, people who have become so desperate for food that they will steal from each other to have something to eat. In the cities they are boiling tulip bulbs and nettles to feed the hungry." The soup kitchens were relief for many people, who did not have the strength to travel. Men, women and children, containers in hand, waited in long lines to get their daily ration of half a liter of broth made from potatoes, cabbage, sugar beets and almost anything else that could pass for food. Even for this you needed food ration coupons! For families that lived in bombed-out houses or air raid shelters, this barely edible soup was the only warm meal that they got because they did not have any fuel for cooking. The Red Cross tried to help, but the Germans, as a retaliatory measure for the railroad strike, refused to cooperate. Only towards the end of the winter did they allow bread from Sweden to be brought in.

To heat their homes, people cut down trees and shrubs in their gardens, the parks and in the streets. Window frames and floorboards were pulled from bombed-out buildings. Even furniture was burnt to get relief from the cold. Many did not make it through the winter, especially the very young and very old.

Besides all this misery there was always the threat of "*razzias*", or round-ups. The Germans would block off a section of a town and search each home, looking for men, Jews and contraband. If they found men, they sent them to labor camps in Germany. If they found a radio; they not only took it away, but then beat the owner before putting him in jail. If they found Jews, they were sent to concentration camps.

The frozen ponds and canals made it possible for the kids to go skating, which is a national sport in Holland. Despite all the suffering, many people still loved to skate. Mr. van Houten still had his old skates, Norwegian long skates, as he called them proudly. The blades were attached to blocks of wood which had the shape of feet. They were tied with long laces underneath the shoes, but some kids wore only socks and tied them directly to their feet. Frans loved to skate and was able to deliver some of the forbidden newspapers that way.

"Come with me to the basement," Mr. van Houten told Frans, "I have to show you something."

Boxes were stacked against one of the walls, all apparently filled with books and old magazines. Mr. van Houten removed some boxes and opened one. He took out a small, homemade radio. He walked to the basement window and pulled out the antenna. He turned the knobs. Suddenly Frans heard a faint sound. It was Radio Orange, with a special program for occupied Holland broadcast by the BBC in London. Frans heard a woman's voice. "It's the Queen," Opa whispered, "Queen Wilhelmina is speaking from London." They both listened intently as the Queen encouraged her people to keep up their spirits. It was the first time that Frans heard Holland's beloved Queen's voice in over four years.

"We will all be free again," the Queen said. "Especially to my countrymen living in the northern part of our country, to you I say hold steadfast, be firm for soon we will all be free again."

"Frans," Mr. van Houten said, "I know you are old enough to keep this an absolute secret. I want you to know that the war is turning in our favor. I have been following the news for some time and I believe that some day we will indeed be free again." Frans, with a lump in his throat, shook Opa's hand. Nothing more was said. They both understood.

One afternoon while skating, Frans saw German soldiers working under one of the canal bridges. He stopped to watch but one of the soldiers pointed his rifle at Frans and told him to go away, and not come back. Frans told Mr. 'K' about it.

"The Germans are placing explosives so they can blow up that bridge when they have to flee from the Allied troops," Mr. 'K' explained, "Tell me exactly what you have seen." From then on Frans reported everything that he saw.

Chapter 10
LIBERATION

Only after the Allied armies had penetrated Germany and were getting close to Berlin, did the Allied Forces resume their effort free the northern part of Holland. On April 20, 1945, the Allied troops tried for a second time to cross the Rhine River near Arnhem.

This time they were successful, but it took days of heavy fighting to take the city. Once they established a foothold in Arnhem, they fought their way northwards. One of the main roads led to Bosdrecht, the town where Frans was living. Mr. 'K' gathered a few men from the Resistance and asked Frans to show them the bridge where the Germans had placed the dynamite. At 10 o'clock that night they gathered at the agreed location. Frans and Geert, whom Frans had met before, went south as look-outs to warn if Germans approached. Two men equipped with cable cutters would float downstream and cut the wires to disconnect the explosives under the bridge. Frans hid underneath shrubbery close to the bridge. Geert went further down the road.

As the fighting came closer, the noise intensified.

The earth trembled and the sky filled with explosions. Out of this inferno a column of German tanks and large trucks thundered northwards. Close to Frans a truck exploded, hit by a projectile that seemed to come out of nowhere. Soldiers jumped screaming from the burning vehicle and ran toward the bridge. A tank pushed the truck aside, and kept going. Fires were everywhere. The smell of burning flesh and rubber choked Frans and the heat scorched his clothes. More vehicles came roaring up the road and across the bridge. It was clear the Germans were fleeing.

Suddenly it was very quiet on the road, although the noise overhead became even louder. A dark green armored car with a white star painted on the front appeared, firing its machine gun northward. It passed Frans, but stopped short of the bridge. Two soldiers got out and took cover low to the ground next to the road, as they slowly crept to the bridge. A jeep with a maple leaf painted on its bumper stopped behind the armored car, an officer got out and spoke with its driver.

Frans jumped up from his hiding place and bolted toward the officer, waving his arms and yelling, "It is safe, it is safe. We cut the cables, we cut the wires!" It took a moment before the officer understood what the boy was saying. Then he smiled and sent two men to check underneath the bridge.

They soon came back, smiling too. "Good job, men. Good job."

The officer suddenly noticed a dark, wet stain on Frans' left shoulder. He touched it with his fingers and exclaimed, "Blood! Boy, you are wounded!" He loosened Frans' jacket and shirt and examined the wound. "A piece of shrapnel hit you. Quick, get in the jeep. I'll bring you back and have a medic take care of this." In the mean time, he unwrapped a bandage and pressed it hard on Frans' shoulder to stop the bleeding. "Since when do they let kids out at night to fight wars?" the officer mumbled to himself. The jeep drove south, passing columns of tanks and trucks until they came to a group of tents in a field along side the road.

The Canadian officer went into one tent while the driver took Frans to another one with a Red Cross flag. The driver told a medic, "Take care of this kid, feed him and find a place for him to sleep, and keep Brigadier Johnson informed about what happens to him."

The medic who started cleaning and dressing Frans' shoulder asked, "Do you know who Brigadier Johnson is?"

"I have no idea," Frans answered.

"Man, he is one of the most important officers in

the Canadian Army."

The pain in his shoulder was not severe, but Frans started to feel faint because of the loss of blood. The medic showed Frans a place where he could lay down. Despite all the noise, Frans fell into a deep sleep, awakening only close to noon the next day.

"We are doing well," the medic said. "Thanks to you guys for saving that bridge. Word has spread that a twelve-year-old has made our rapid advance possible."

"But that is not true," Frans said. "I was only a lookout. The men from the Resistance cut the cables. Have you seen any of them?" Frans asked.

"Not that I know of. Hopefully they got away in time. Whatever happened to them, to us you are a hero," the medic replied.

Later that afternoon Brigadier Johnson came by and asked Frans how he was doing.

"I am fine," Frans answered. "The wound will heal soon, I have been told."

"Why don't you come with me to headquarters in Arnhem? You speak English so well, we can use a few more interpreters."

Frans was sitting next to Brigadier Johnson as the jeep sped south, in the direction of Arnhem, with soldiers saluting as they drove by. Brigadier Johnson and his aide were constantly on their radios, listening and giving orders. Arriving at his headquarters, a half-burned-out hotel, the Brigadier told one of his aides, "Take care of this young man, make sure he gets what he needs and then bring him to the translators' room. Tell Captain Walsh that I sent him." He pointed his finger at Frans. "You and I will have dinner tonight. Wait for me there." And off he went.

Frans asked the aide, Rickey, if he could make a phone call to try and reach his parents.

"Sorry, but the phone lines are still out. Can't help you there," he said.

Downstairs, in what used to be the restaurant, soldiers seated behind tables were talking to locals with the help of interpreters Frans was glad to notice that he was not the only young person. There were other teenagers, both boys and girls, assisting the soldiers. The most frequently asked questions by the Dutch civilians were, how they might find family members who were missing, where they might stay for the night, and where to get food or medical help? Though a lot of Dutchmen spoke some English, Frans was able to help many others in communicating with the Canadians.

It was already dark when a voice rang out, "Frans, Brigadier Johnson wants to see you."

"Let's go to the mess hall and have dinner," Brigadier Johnson said. He listened attentively as

Frans told his story. The officer kept asking for more and more details.

"Do you know how your parents are?" he asked. Frans said that he had not heard anything since he had run away with Bill.

Brigadier Johnson looked Frans in the eyes and said firmly, "We will get you to them, I promise, just give it some time. Your parents must be proud of you, you acted like a man and helped us substantially." Frans blushed, but at the same time felt happy. "How about your friend Bill? Do you know what regiment he belonged to?" the Brigadier continued.

"He told me that he is an American Air Force major and a squadron commander, and gave me his serial number, which will tell you who he is."

"We will find him, if he is still alive." Brigadier Johnson said. That thought alone made Frans shudder. He realized that many people had died, but hopefully nobody who was as close to him as Bill. The next few days he stayed at headquarters. He ate in the mess hall and slept in the hotel's banquet room. It was crowded, with more than forty men sleeping there, but now Frans no longer minded.

One morning Brigadier Johnson told that Frans could go on a transport to Nijmegen. "Tomorrow morning a car will pick you up," the Brigadier said. "Be ready at eight, and make sure to keep this note with you. Whenever you need help, like food or transportation, show this to an officer. You'll be surprised what it will do."

Chapter 11
HOME AGAIN

While waiting for his ride the next morning, Frans kept thinking about how long it had been since he had seen his parents. It had been over a year, but he felt many years older. All sorts of questions raced through his head. How had they managed during all this time? Would they be home? Was their house damaged like so many others were?

Nearing Nijmegen, Frans was mortified by all the destruction. He barely recognized the city. As the jeep turned the corner of his street all he could see was ruins. Not one house was left standing. Frans panicked. "What happened? What happened?" he yelled out. The street was abandoned. There was nobody that could hear him, nobody that could answer him. Frans felt totally devastated. He sat on the rubble and cried uncontrollable

"Where is my Mom? Where is my Dad?" he kept repeating to himself.

The driver asked, "Do you have any other family? Aunts or uncles where I can take you? I'll bring you there. Do you have an address?" Frans thought of his aunt and uncle who lived on the edge of town, and he told the driver about them.

Driving through his hometown, Frans realized how much had been destroyed. When they found the street where his aunt lived, Frans was relieved to see that at least her house was still standing. At first he did not dare to ring the doorbell, afraid of what he might learn. After he finally rang the bell, it took a long time before he heard footsteps in the hallway.

His aunt opened the door. She let out a scream. "Annie! Come! Your son is here!" Frans barely recognized the woman who ran up to him and embraced him. She seemed so much smaller. Her hair was grey. She looked so thin. She loosened her grip to look at him and cried even harder.

"Thank God, finally you're back. I missed you. I have missed you so much." Frans' mother kept crying, and held him tight while they entered the living room.

"I came here because I thought you might be staying here since our house is gone. Where is Dad?" he asked. There was no answer. Now his aunt cried also."Where is Dad?" Frans asked again.

"Dad is no more," his Mom finally stuttered, "he is gone." Slowly the truth began to sink in. My Dad is gone. How can that be? I need my Dad. Frans started to cry again. This time it seemed like he would never stop. For all that had happened, he never thought that he would lose a parent. He felt more miserable than he ever had at any time during his life.

"What happened?" he kept asking. "What happened?" Frans heard the story in bits and pieces.

Frans' father had previously worked as a clerk at a hospital. A short time after Frans left for boarding school, he switched jobs to work in the wards with the patients. This work was considered indispensable, and exempted him from being sent to Germany. Later he worked as a medical orderly on ambulances.

Then in September, the Americans came down from the sky. Everybody was so happy, happy to be free, but the Germans fought back, and shelled the town. "Your father was on a ambulance, and was rescuing a victim from a burning building when a wall collapsed. Your Dad was very seriously hurt. The doctors did everything they could, but he died two days later."

"And our house?" asked Frans, "what happened to our house?"

"Nobody knows for sure," his aunt replied. "A fire started on one end of the street, and with so much fighting going on, in no time the entire block went up in flames. There was nothing the fire brigade could do. Your mother lost practically everything that she owned. With your father gone, you missing, and then losing her house, she fell into a deep depression, and was unable to work."

Frans embraced his mother. The sorrow he felt for her was greater than his own. The following days were spent talking. He told his mother how he had managed, and how so many people had been good to him, about Opa and Oma and especially his American friend Bill, whom he hoped so much to see again.

"You can stay here," his aunt said, "but since we don't have another bedroom you'll have to sleep in the attic."

"Thank you for all you have done for Mom and me," Frans said. "We will stay in Nijmegen, and Mom and I will start looking for a small apartment or a few rooms in a house." The war had turned his life upside down. Frans realized he now had to take care of his mother.

Chapter 12
REUNION

Frans went looking for the Canadian headquarters. As soon as he showed the guard Brigadier Johnson's note, he was quickly allowed in. A radio operator went to work and within half an hour Frans was talking to Brigadier Johnson.

"I have good news," the Brigadier said. "Bill is OK. He got hurt a bit, but nothing that time won't heal. He will be shipped back to the States in a few weeks. He is in Maastricht, and if you want to see him you had better go soon. Let me know if you need help getting there."

"Can my Mom also go with me?" Frans asked.

"Of course she can," the Brigadier answered. "Take her with you and give my regards to Bill, for he sounds like an OK guy." He certainly is, Frans thought.

The next morning, a large truck picked up Frans and his Mom in front of the train station. His Mom sat in front next to the driver, and Frans climbed in the back where he joined a group of soldiers.

In Maastricht the truck stopped at the entrance of a hospital. Frans was confused. "This is the address I was given," the driver said. "Hop out, I've got to keep moving."

At the reception desk a nurse told Frans what room to go to. Frans hesitated to enter. When he finally did, he saw Bill in bed with his right arm and leg in traction. A big smile appeared on Bill's face. "Look who is here!" he exclaimed, "the man who saved my life. Hey guys," he called out loudly, "this is Frans, the guy I have been talking about."

All the men, as best as they could, applauded and yelled their hellos. Frans, embarrassed as he was, hugged Bill and then introduced his Mom. "Man, I am glad to see you. I knew you would make it. Tell me everything," Bill said.

"But what happened to you? Are you seriously wounded?" Frans asked.

"Its not as bad as it looks," Bill answered, and started to tell what happened to him after they had last seen each other on the farm. Bill had helped to blow up some buildings, laid mines near German installations, and other similar activities.

"How did you get wounded?" Frans asked.

"Nothing to do with the war, actually," Bill said. "The jeep which I was driving ran off the road, but I'll be all right. At least I can go home. In about two weeks they fly me to England, and from there by boat to the States. By that time I should be up and running again. I'll be home with my family." Bill was ever so happy with that prospect.

"You, Frans, and your Mom will have to come and visit me. You have to promise me that. I'll be at our farm, since my father is now 68 and really wants to retire. I'll be a farmer, man, and that is what I want to be. From now on I will stay home and work the land. I am lucky to have come out alive. The kids, Marie and Mickey, have grown so much. I am sure they all want to meet you."

Frans and Bill talked for hours. Frans had never before experienced what it meant to have such a close friend. When he finally left, he promised again to visit Bill. . .

"Till we meet in the States."